For Danielle,
Dec. 25, 2003

The Maid and the Mouse
and the Odd-shaped House

To Joan Sugarman —

all best wishes,

Paul O. Zelinsky

From: Grandmother

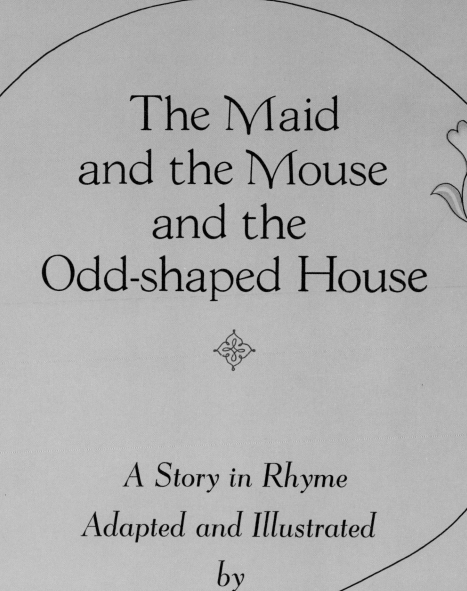

The Maid
and the Mouse
and the
Odd-shaped House

A Story in Rhyme

Adapted and Illustrated

by

Paul O. Zelinsky

DODD, MEAD & CO.

NEW YORK

The Maid and the Mouse and the Odd-shaped House was adapted from a rhyming story written in the 1897 notebook of Jane Henriette Holzer, a schoolteacher in Bridgeport, Connecticut. Its authorship is unknown, although in format it is based on a "tell and draw story" found both in American and English folk literature. As the story was used in Miss Holzer's classroom, a different child would go to the chalkboard to add each successive part to the picture as it was called for in the text.

The artist would like to thank Mrs. Dorothy Brooks for finding the story in her mother's notebook.

3   4   5   6   7   8   9   10

Library of Congress Cataloging in Publication Data

Zelinsky, Paul O
The maid and the mouse and the odd-shaped house.

SUMMARY: An oddly-shaped house takes on the
appearance of a cat as the maid and mouse who live there
make various changes in it.
[1.   Dwellings—Fiction.   2.   Mice—Fiction.
3.   Stories in rhyme]   I.   Title.
PZ8.3.Z34Mai   [E]   80-2774
ISBN 0-396-07938-5

For my mother and father
with love

Once in a funny, odd-shaped house
There lived a wee maid and a mouse.
The mouse was fat, the maid was thin.
The house was new—they'd just moved in.

In this first picture you will see
The house they lived in happily.

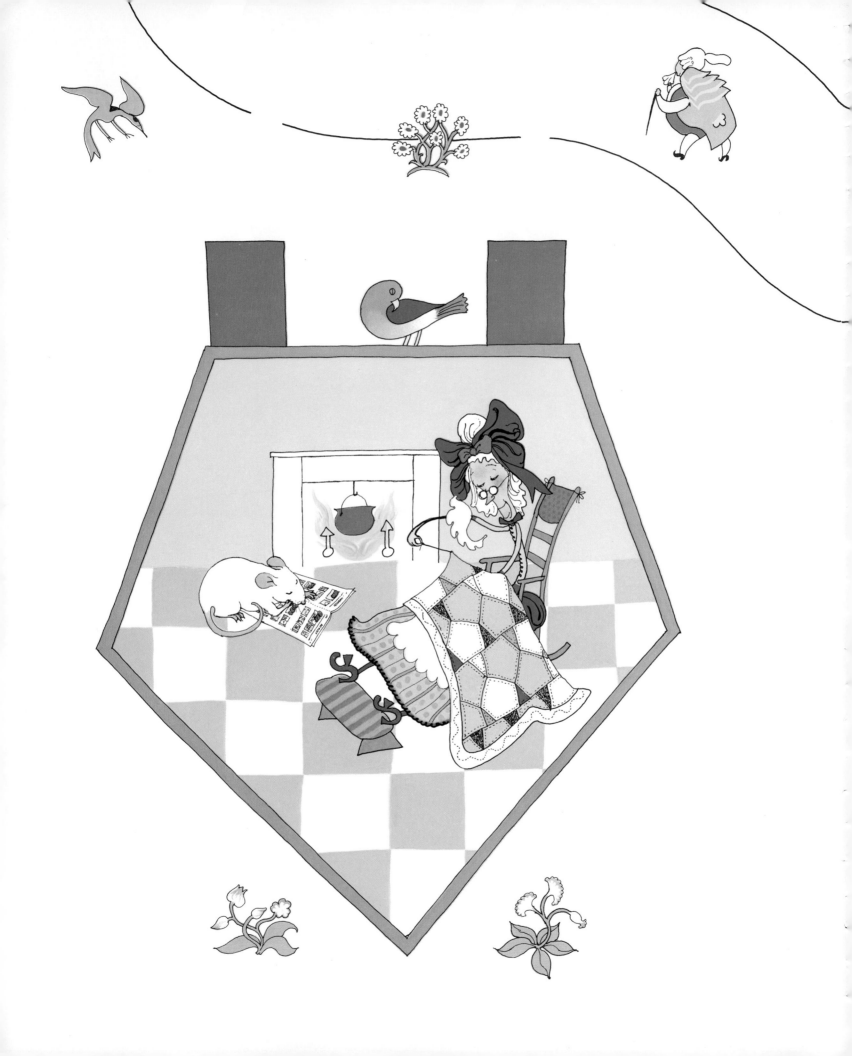

Things were fine until they tried
To build a fire. The wee maid cried,
"I'm very much afraid we'll choke
With no place to let out the smoke."

With care they reached the roof and laid
Red bricks with mortar. Soon they'd made
Two chimneys—sturdy, fireproof,
A proud addition to the roof.

Now in this picture all is well.
The chimneys work, as you can tell.

Then the maid said to the mouse,
"Let's build four rooms inside our house.
One room for me and one for you;
Our guests can use the other two."

The mouse agreed, and here you find
Four simple rooms that they designed.

"Oh, what a grand and splendid place!"
The wee maid said. "What style! What grace!
And yet it needs"—she stroked her chin—
"I know! Let's put two windows in.
We'll stand behind them, snug and sly,
And peek out at the passersby."

"Good!" said the mouse, and here the two
Are slyly peeking out at you.

One yellowish September day
(The guests had come and gone away)
The wee maid said, "I'm sure I hear
A nasty hissing somewhere near.
You stay at home and guard the house;
I'll go see what it is, dear Mouse."

So while the mouse secured the door,
The wee maid set out to explore.

She tiptoed nimbly for a spell—
Then tripped and fell! And tripped and fell!
In tears she rose and tiptoed when—
Oh, no! She tripped and fell again!
And *then* she heard a dreadful roar.

She hardly dared to rise once more.
But up she got—and down she fell!
A sad, sad tale it is to tell.

This is the path the wee maid took.
This is the way her tumbles look.

"I've had enough," the wee maid said.
"I've hurt my nose and bumped my head.
Nor can I tell what made that sound.
I don't see anything around."

She headed home, and here's the track
She made as she was going back.

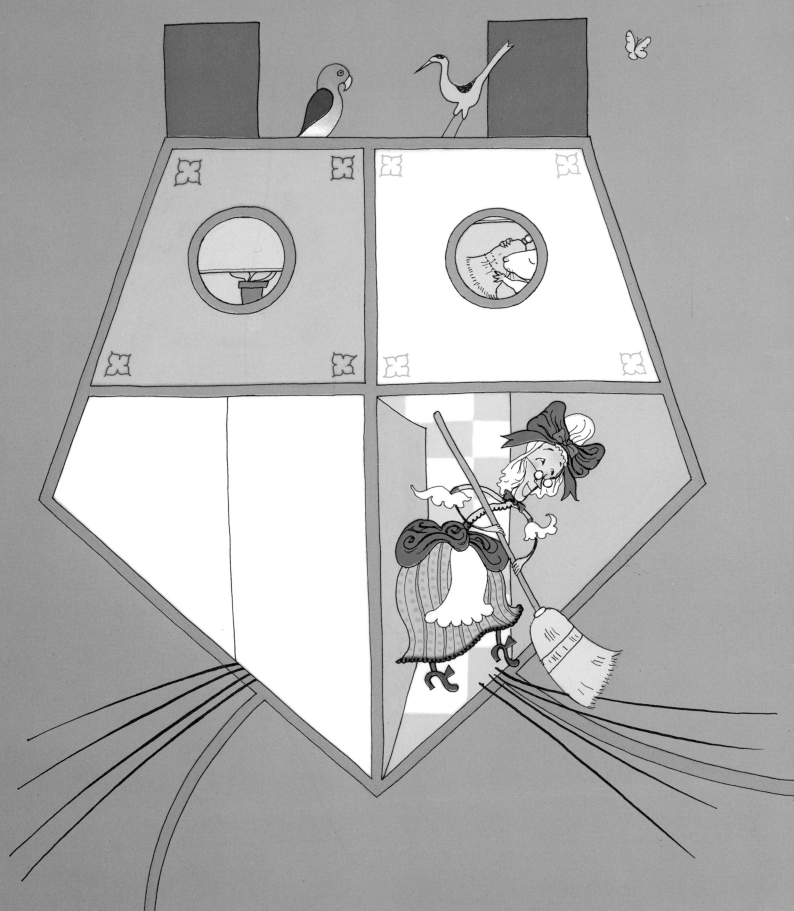

The maid said, "I've searched far and wide."
"But not indoors," the mouse replied.
"Suppose we clean the house and look
In every corner, every nook."
So mouse with whisk and maid with broom
Went carefully through every room.

They swept and swept and swept the floors;
The dirt went streaming out the doors.

Then out the door the wee maid stepped.
She said, "The garden path's not swept.
I'll do it now." She rolled her sleeves
And brushed away the fallen leaves.

And when the fallen leaves were cleared
This is the way the path appeared.

She'd scarcely finished working when
She heard that dreadful roar again!
She turned. Her eyes grew big and black.
Her legs shot up, her hands flew back.
"What is the matter?" called the mouse
As she came running toward the house.

"Matter enough, my mouse so fat!
Oh, dear! Alas! It is the CAT!"

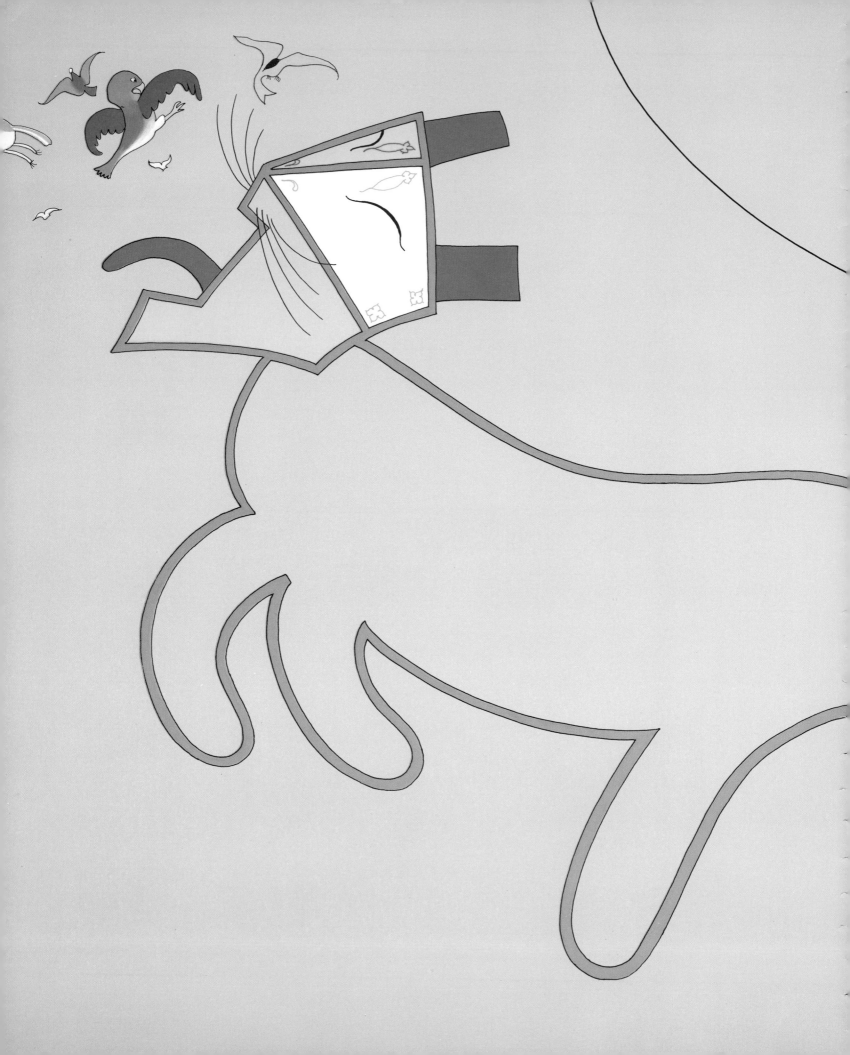

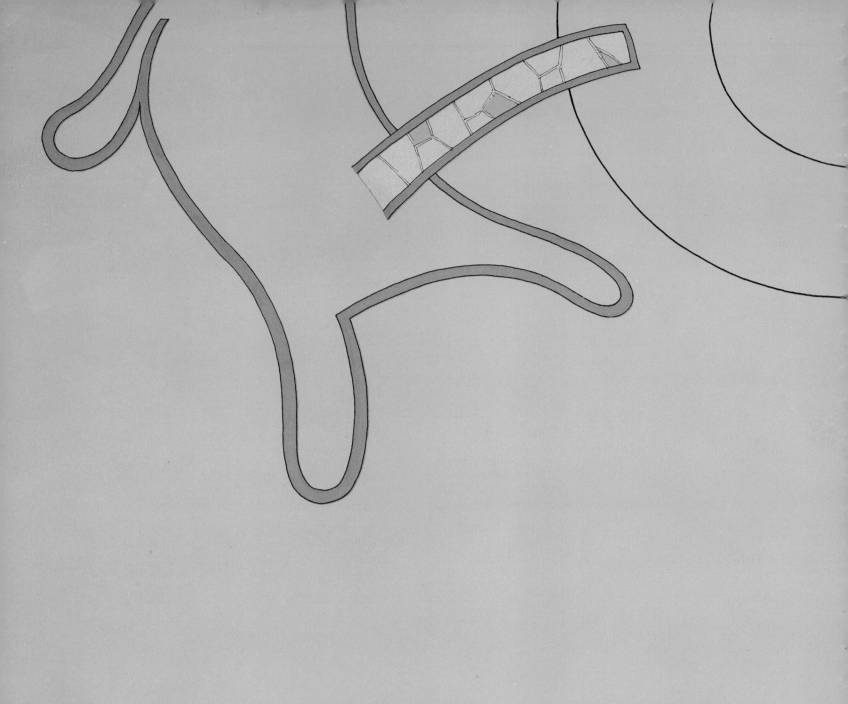

And now you see them safe and sound;
No noise disturbs the house they found.
There's nothing here that's odd at all.
You're welcome if you come to call.